W9-BIQ-758

SOLD!

by Diana G. Gallagher

illustrated by Brann Garvey

Claudia Cristina Cortez is published by Stone Arch Books
151 Good Counsel Drive, P.O. Box 669
Mankato, Minnesota 56002
www.stonearchbooks.com

Copyright © 2010 by Stone Arch Books

All rights reserved. No part of this publication may be reproduced
in whole or in part, or stored in a retrieval system, or transmitted in any
form or by any means, electronic, mechanical, photocopying, recording,
or otherwise, without written permission of the publisher.

Library of Congress Cataloging-in-Publication Data
Gallagher, Diana G.
  Sold! / by Diana G. Gallagher ; illustrated by Brann Garvey.
    p. cm. — (Claudia Cristina Cortez)
  ISBN 978-1-4342-1572-7
  [1. Rummage sales—Fiction. 2. Middle schools—Fiction. 3. Schools—Fiction.
4. Hispanic Americans—Fiction.] I. Garvey, Brann, ill. II. Title.
  PZ7.G13543So 2010
  [Fic]—dc22
                                2009002543

Summary:
Claudia's class needs to earn money for a field trip, so they're holding a rummage
sale. Anna's team challenges Claudia's to a contest. Who can raise the most money
and sell the most stuff? Anna and her friends are selling fashionable clothes, but
Claudia thinks her team's quirky collectibles have a chance.

Creative Director: Heather Kindseth
Graphic Designer: Carla Zetina-Yglesias

Photo Credits
Delaney Photography, cover

Printed in the United States of America

R0431118725

Table of Contents

Cast of

ME

CLAUDIA
That's me. I'm thirteen, and I'm in the seventh grade at Pine Tree Middle School. I live with my mom, my dad, and my brother, Jimmy. I have one cat, Ping-Ping. I like music, baseball, and hanging out with my friends.

MONICA is my very best friend. We met when we were really little, and we've been best friends ever since. I don't know what I'd do without her! Monica loves horses. In fact, when she grows up, she wants to be an Olympic rider!

MONICA

BECCA

BECCA is one of my closest friends. She lives next door to Monica. Becca is really, really smart. She gets good grades. She's also really good at art.

ADAM and I met when we were in third grade. Now that we're teenagers, we don't spend as much time together as we did when we were kids, but he's always there for me when I need him. (Plus, he's the only person who wants to talk about baseball with me!)

ADAM

Characters

TOMMY's our class clown. Sometimes he's really funny, but sometimes he is just annoying. Becca has a crush on him . . . but I'd never tell.

I think **PETER** is probably the smartest person I've ever met. Seriously. He's even smarter than our teachers! He's also one of my friends. Which is lucky, because sometimes he helps me with homework.

Every school has a bully, and **JENNY** is ours. She's the tallest person in our class, and the meanest, too. She always threatens to stomp people. No one's ever seen her stomp anyone, but that doesn't mean it hasn't happened!

ANNA is the most popular girl at our school. Everyone wants to be friends with her. I think that's weird, because Anna can be really, really mean. I mostly try to stay away from her.

Cast of

CARLY

CARLY is Anna's best friend. She always tries to act exactly like Anna does. She even wears the exact same clothes. She's never really been mean to me, but she's never been nice to me either!

SYLVIA really wants to be best friends with Anna, but Anna isn't very nice to her. I'm not very close with Sylvia, but she's always pretty nice to me and my friends.

SYLVIA

BRAD

BRAD is our school's football star. He's also really, really cute. Becca and Monica know that I have a secret crush on him. I hope they never tell anyone!

Characters

NICK is my annoying seven-year-old neighbor. I get stuck babysitting him a lot. He likes to make me miserable. (Okay, he's not that bad ALL of the time . . . just most of the time.)

NICK

JIMMY

JIMMY is my big brother. I stay out of his way, and he stays out of mine. (But sometimes he does give me some pretty good advice.)

UNCLE DIEGO is my dad's brother. He comes over a lot, usually to eat a meal with my family. I really like Uncle Diego. He's funny, and he treats me like an adult, not like a little kid.

UNCLE DIEGO

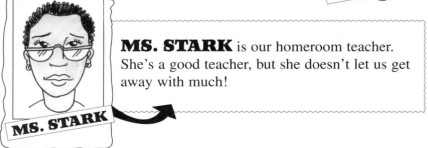

MS. STARK

MS. STARK is our homeroom teacher. She's a good teacher, but she doesn't let us get away with much!

CHAPTER 1

FIELD TRIP

Anna Dunlap, the most popular girl at my school, can take the fun out of anything. She says you're a **middle school loser** if you:

1. Watch Saturday morning cartoons.

2. Enjoy shopping with your mom.

3. Put yellow mustard on hot dogs.

She also thinks that:

1. Ice cream = pimples.

2. Roller blades = thick ankles.

3. Video games = brain rot.

I love ice cream, rollerblades, and video games. I also like yellow mustard, cartoons, and shopping with my mom, and **I don't care what Anna thinks**.

Anna thinks she's better than everyone else, and she never misses a chance to prove it.

I never pass up a chance to prove her **wrong**.

Like the day she turned the class rummage sale into a contest to see who had the 𝔅𝔈𝔖𝒯 used stuff.

Every year, the Pine Tree Middle School seventh grade visits a historical park called Old Town. People there wear colonial costumes and show how early Americans lived and worked.

The field trip is one of the best parts of seventh grade, but **it's not free**. So every year, the class holds a rummage sale to raise money to pay for tickets and lunch.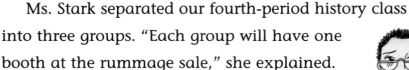

Ms. Stark separated our fourth-period history class into three groups. "Each group will have one booth at the rummage sale," she explained.

I waved to my friends. Becca, Monica, Adam, Tommy, and Peter came to my desk.

Carly Madison and four other girls rushed over to Anna. They reminded me of *hungry flies* zooming in on a garbage dump. They want to be popular, and Anna is the most popular girl in school. Some girls would do almost **anything** if Anna said it was cool.

Larry Kyle doesn't want to be friends with Anna. She always **teases him** for being short. That's why I was surprised when Larry walked over and stood with Anna's group.

"What are you doing?" Anna asked, loud enough for the whole class to hear.

"You need one more person," Larry told her.

There are twenty-one kids in our history class. **21 kids divided by 3 = 7 kids per group.**

"I don't need you," Anna said. She paused. She didn't care if **she hurt Larry's feelings**, but she knew Ms. Stark wouldn't like it. She tried to think up a good reason. "Because, um — well . . . uh . . ."

That's how I sound when I try to talk to Brad Turino. He's my school's gorgeous sports star, and I have a **secret crush** on him. I can't even say "Hello, Brad." I stumble over the words.

"Well — because we're going to sell clothes," Anna said finally. "Do you know anything about *girls' clothes?*"

"No," Larry said. He frowned.

"Or perfume?" Karen Chen added. "My mom is donating dozens of sample bottles."

"And I'm bringing lots of earrings," Carly said. "Are your ears pierced?"

"Forget it!" Larry said. He slapped his hands over his ears. Then he joined Brad's group in the corner.

That left Sylvia Slother and Jenny Pinski, the bully, still standing by their desks.

I knew that **Sylvia** was just **too shy** to join Anna's group, even though she really wanted Anna to like her.

Ms. Stark put Sylvia in my group, so we had seven.

Anna got **Jenny**. She looked upset, but she couldn't kick Jenny out, because:

A. Ms. Stark wouldn't allow it.

B. Jenny might get mad.

C. If Jenny got mad, who knows what could happen.

Nobody wanted to make Jenny mad. Not even Anna. But **Anna** loved to pick on everyone else.

"I bet our booth makes the most money," Anna said. "We might even **beat the school record**. My designer clothes are worth a lot."

"It doesn't matter how much each group makes," I told her. "All the money goes together to pay for the field trip."

Anna shrugged. Then she said, "A contest would make the rummage sale more interesting, but *if you're afraid*, we don't have to do it."

"We're not afraid," **Adam** said.

"Not even a little," Monica agreed. She's my best friend, and she doesn't care what Anna thinks either.

"Not at all," Tommy said. "Who wants to buy your **old clothes** anyway?"

All the girls — except Becca, Monica, Jenny, and me — raised their hands.

Anna has fantastic clothes. **She probably would make more money.**

Still, we couldn't turn down the challenge.

"**You're on,**" I said. "Whoever makes the most money at their booth wins."

Anna grinned.

CHAPTER 2

SALES STRATEGY

My rummage sale group met in my back yard after school.

Usually, my friends and I hung out in the tree house. But there wasn't really room for seven kids in the tree house, so we sat on the grass instead. **Ping-ping,** my Siamese cat, curled up in my lap.

Monica started things off. "We need a plan to beat Anna," she said.

"Definitely," I agreed.

The back door of my house slammed, and Nick ran out. He's the **seven-year-old brat** who lives next door. My mom watches him when his mom has something to do.

I usually get STUCK with him. Sometimes Mom pays me. **Sometimes she doesn't.**

"Hey, Claudia!" **Nick** yelled.

Ping-ping hissed and jumped out of my lap. She scrambled up a tree and hid.

Nick is **#1 on Ping-ping's list of horrible things to avoid**. She'd rather go to the vet and eat rotten fish heads than let Nick near her. He poured maple syrup on her tail two years ago. Cats do not like sticky fur or baths.

Nick plopped down on the ground next to Becca. He never asks if he can be near us, and there's no point telling him to get lost.

If you do:

First Nick gets mad.

Next he throws a fit.

Then he gets even.

Nick is good at getting even. I learned that the hard way. **He has:**

1. Ripped up my homework.

2. Smeared peanut butter in my hair.

3. Thrown away my shoes.

There's more, but it would take too long to write everything down. I'm just glad my friends don't mind **noşy little kidş.**

"What are you doing?" Nick asked.

Adam answered, "We have to sell a bunch of 𝔍𝔘𝔑𝔎 so we can go to Old Town."

"What's Old Town?" Nick asked.

"A historical site," **Peter** said. "It's a field trip the seventh grade goes on every year. At Old Town, everything is set up like it was two hundred years ago. It's very **educational.**"

"They don't have electricity," Monica said. "They use lanterns and candles."

"People make the candles right there," I said. My brother, Jimmy, told me all about Old Town after his class went three years ago. "They use braided cotton wicks and animal fat to make the candles."

"Animal fat is called tallow," Peter explained. He's the smartest kid at Pine Tree Middle School. **I think he knows everything.**

"I want to see how they turn wool into thread on a spinning wheel," Becca said.

"I want to watch the blacksmith pound **red-hot metal** into horseshoes and shovels," Adam said.

"I want to **get out of school** for a day," Tommy said, laughing.

"I want to go!" Nick exclaimed.

"You can go," **Sylvia** said. "When  you're in seventh grade."

"I want to go now," Nick said. He frowned. It looked like he was about to have a 𝕋𝔸ℕ𝕋ℝ𝕌𝕄.

Uh-oh. Nick's tantrums are on my list of horrible things to avoid. They're worse  than **stepping on anthills with bare feet.**

"We have to write reports about it," I said.

"That's not fun!" Nick said. He threw up his hands.

"Not much," I said. It wasn't exactly true, but the little lie worked. Nick stopped wanting to go to Old Town. The problem was that he didn't run out of questions. Seven-year-olds never run out of questions.

"Then why are you selling stuff so that you can go?" Nick asked.

"The rummage sale will be F𝕌ℕ," Becca said.

"Even if Anna's group makes more money," Monica agreed.

"We can beat Anna and Carly," Adam said. He played baseball and football. **He hated to lose.**

"We just have to sell **better stuff** than Anna's old clothes," Tommy said.

"Everything is better than clothes," Nick said.

"Not if you're a **teenager**," I explained.

"The rummage sale is open to everyone," Peter pointed out. "Not just kids from school."

"We still need some cool stuff to compete with Anna," Monica said.

"I've got a bunch of extra comics we can sell," Adam said.

Nick looked up. "Do you have any **Viper Man**?" he asked.

"A few," Adam said. "Do you like *Star Voyages*?"

Nick shook his head. "Boring."

"My dad loves *Star Voyages*," Tommy said. "He has all the books and DVDs. He even has **a complete set** of the plastic drink cups they gave away at Captain Chicken."

"That's how we can beat Anna!" I exclaimed. "We'll sell things people like to collect."

"That won't be hard," Monica said. "People collect some pretty **weird stuff**."

"No kidding," Peter said. He rolled his eyes. "My uncle has a closet full of baseball caps. He never wears them, but he won't let my aunt get rid of them. He buys new ones all the time, too."

"My uncle Diego always says that **one man's junk is another man's treasure**," I said. "I guess that's the kind of thing he meant."

"That's true," Tommy agreed. "Our garage is like a gigantic junk drawer. It's packed with stuff my mom buys at garage sales."

"My mom loves garage sales," Becca said. "She comes home all EXCITED because she only paid fifty cents for this or a dollar for that."

"So we should keep our prices low," Monica said.

"Maybe," I said. "But then we'll have to sell a ton of stuff to beat Anna's team."

"That's what we should call our booth," Sylvia said. **"Tons of Stuff."**

CHAPTER 3

MORE STUFF

The next day at school, Anna didn't stop BRAGGING. She kept telling everyone about how she and her friends had some **fabulous** clothes and accessories to sell. All of it came from their closets.

I was at **my locker** before homeroom when Anna and her friends walked over to Anna's locker. It was pretty close to mine.

"I'm selling a Ginger Snap shoulder bag," Anna said. "**It doesn't match** any of my outfits."

"I'll buy it!" Linda Dint shouted.

"*No fair,*" another girl complained. "I've always wanted a Ginger Snap bag."

"It's orange and blue," Carly said. "It doesn't match anything."

Linda shrugged. "**I don't care,**" she said. "I want it anyway."

Anna shook her head. "**No sales** until Saturday," she said. "We have to make the money at the rummage sale or it won't count for the school record."

"Which we're going to 𝔹ℝ𝔼𝔸𝕂," Carly added with a smug smile.

"Are you selling your pink Carolina sandals, Carly?" Kristin asked.

"I might," Carly said. "For the **right price**, of course."

Anna caught me watching. "Do you have anything **fabulous** to sell yet, Claudia?" she asked.

"Lots," I lied. "But you'll have to wait and be surprised." I hid my list so Anna couldn't peek. My stuff was **lame** compared to her cast-offs.

Claudia's Rummage Sale Donations

Mom: jewelry, clothes, pots and dishes

Dad: puzzle game, executive desktop golf set

Uncle Diego: CDs, T-shirts

Actually, my list was **worse than lame.** I probably couldn't give some of my stuff away.

Only another **mom** would want my mom's clothes and jewelry.

The coffee pot had a small dent, and it wasn't even the kind that plugged in.

All the dishes were mismatched. Nobody would want those.

The puzzle and golf games had never been opened. Dad gets weird gifts because **nobody knows what he wants**. He doesn't want games. Maybe somebody else would.

I didn't know any of the music groups on Uncle Diego's CDs. They were **old guys**.

The T-shirts were new, but they all had ads on the front. My uncle got them from grand openings and radio contests. The T-shirts said things like:

Eat Greg's Great Chicken!

Wake up with WCJT! We're LOUD in the morning!

My big brother, Jimmy, didn't want to give anything away. **I didn't want to beg.** I just reminded him that I donated some of my Darling Ponies for his seventh-grade rummage sale.

My friends didn't have a lot of L𝒰𝒞𝒦 with their families, either.

Later that day, Anna stood behind my friends and me in the lunch line.

"I'm selling two pairs of K Brand jeans," Anna told us. "Bet you can't beat that."

"My dad's old tools are a lot better," Adam said.

Anna laughed and said, "I don't think so."

"Guys like old tools, Anna," I argued.

"But how much will they pay?" Anna asked. She didn't wait for an answer. She just **rolled her eyes** and walked away.

"I guess Anna wouldn't be impressed with the **cute baby things** my aunt donated," Becca said.

"Or my step-sister's stuffed animals," Monica added.

"We need **better stuff**," I said.

Adam nodded. "And **more of it**," he said nervously.

CHAPTER 4

STOCKING UP

Everyone in the Tons of Stuff group was hunting for SUPER STUFF. Anna would gloat for weeks if she and her friends made more money than we did.

Gloating = being too happy about winning, and rubbing it in to the losers

The dreaded Anna Dunlap Gloat is on everyone's **Horrible-Things-To-Avoid** list.

The Anna Dunlap Gloat

1. Anna points.

2. Anna laughs.

3. Anna whispers behind your back.

Bonus: Her friends giggle when they see you.

The rummage sale wasn't as much fun anymore. It was **serious business.** That was my fault for taking the **dare**, but nobody wanted to back out. We were in it to win it.

I had to get serious about getting more stuff to sell. After school, I headed out to ask my neighbors for donations.

First, I knocked on Mrs. Arnold's door. I walk her dog sometimes, so I've been in her house a lot. I knew that it was **loaded** with knick-knacks, books, and pictures.

"My class is having a rummage sale to pay for our field trip to Old Town," I explained. "Do you have anything to donate to the sale? **I'd really appreciate it.**"

Hint: Grown-ups love to help if:

1. You're doing something for school.

2. You're polite.

3. You're very, very grateful.

"I'd love to help, Claudia," Mrs. Arnold said, "but I'm having my own garage sale, so I need to keep my things. **I'm sorry.**"

"When is your garage sale?" I asked nervously. I hoped it wasn't the same day as the seventh-grade rummage sale.

"Next summer," Mrs. Arnold said.

Whew! That was a RELIEF.

Hint: When grown-ups say no:

1. Say you understand.

2. Nod and sigh.

3. Then smile sadly.

I did all of the above. It worked. Mrs. Arnold gave me some holiday potholders and six mugs with funny sayings.

Mrs. Pike usually gives her old things to the Animal Shelter Thrift Store, but **she likes me**, because sometimes I help her with her garden. She gave me some cute glass cats, a flower painting, and a box of old records.

"I've never seen records like these," I said, looking into the box. They weren't as big as Uncle Diego's old records.

"These records are called 78s," Mrs. Pike explained. "You need an *antique* crank-up record player to hear them."

"Thank you," I said, smiling. I knew that no one would buy old records they couldn't play, but **I didn't want to hurt her feelings.**

I saved Mr. and Mrs. Gomez for last. They live across the street from my house. They gave me board games, craft kits, and some of Fancy's old coats and collars.

Fancy is a poodle. Mrs. Gomez feeds her **gourmet dog food** and buys her expensive toys and clothes. Mrs. Gomez loves Fancy more than anything. Mr. Gomez loves golfing and taking care of his lawn.

Hint: Grown-ups spend money on hobbies.

"You should come to our rummage sale, Mr. Gomez," I said. "We have an executive desktop golf game to sell. **It's brand new.**"

Mr. Gomez's eyes lit up.

Sold!

I hoped some other dog lovers would pay a lot for Fancy's designer dog clothes. So far, they were the best things I had for the sale.

CHAPTER 5

EVERYBODY'S JUNK

Ms. Stark taught us that every sale has three parts.

1. Stocking

2. Inventory and pricing

3. Selling

By Thursday afternoon, my group was mostly done with Part 1. We brought our stuff to Adam's house for Part 2. His garage was the Tons of Stuff warehouse.

I hauled my things over to Adam's in Mom's garden wagon. I parked it by the pile of **bags and boxes** in the garage.

"Wow!" Peter exclaimed. "That's a lot of junk."

"**Treasure** junk or just junk?" Tommy asked.

"We have to look at everything to find out," Monica said.

"I'll make a list," Sylvia said. She sat on a plastic chair and opened a small notebook.

"I brought little stickers for prices," Becca said. "We can write prices on them." She held up a packet of white circle stickers.

Adam pointed to a stack of cardboard boxes. "Peter and I will sort and pack," he said.

"I'm ready to mark prices," I said. I held up a pen. So did Monica.

"Too bad we're not being graded," Peter said. "We'd get **extra credit** for being organized."

"No credit!" Tommy said, wagging his finger. "Cash only."

Everyone laughed. Tommy is the class clown. He isn't always funny, but that was a **good joke**.

We got started. Becca and Tommy took turns holding up each item, and Sylvia wrote down everything we had in her notebook. Then we set a price.

We did **not** always agree on how much to ask.

"**Three dollars** for this?" Tommy asked, frowning. He dangled a fashion doll by the hair.

"Careful!" Becca said. She took the doll and fluffed its blond curls. "My aunt would pay five dollars if this doll had **pink hair**."

"It comes with three outfits," Monica said. "Three dollars is a **steal**."

"If you say so," Tommy said doubtfully. He grabbed something else from a cardboard box.

A little voice said, "**Hello. Let's count to ten!**"

Tommy pulled out a toy cell phone. The buttons lit up.

"Cool!" Tommy said. "They didn't make these when I was a little kid."

"You can have it now," Adam joked. "For five bucks."

"Isn't that too much?" I asked. "It's just a **used** plastic toy."

"Ask for five dollars, but if someone offers us three dollars, **we'll take it**," Peter suggested.

"I don't want it," Tommy said. He handed the toy to me. I put a $5.00 sticker on it and gave it to Adam.

"We should make all the prices a little high," Monica said. "My grandma always **tries to bargain** when she buys stuff at yard sales."

"So does mine," I said, "unless it's something with Cranky Cat on it. Then she just buys it **no matter how expensive it is**. My grandma really likes that cartoon cat."

"This cartoon cat?" Tommy asked. He held up a small flower pot. It had a picture of **Cranky Cat** sitting next to a wilted flower.

"Yes!" I exclaimed. "I don't think Grandma has a Cranky Cat flower pot. How much?"

Tommy thought for a second. *"Ten dollars!"* he yelled.

That was definitely too much. "Three dollars," I said.

"Five and it's **yours**," Tommy said, holding out the pot.

"Four," I said. "And that's my **final** offer."

"Going, going, gone!" Tommy said. He grinned.

"That was great!" Monica said, clapping her hands. "We'll have to do that at the rummage sale. People L♡VE to bargain about prices."

I knew she was right — especially if they get a good deal. I would have paid five dollars for the flower pot, but **I didn't say so.**

Becca put a "sold" sticker on the pot and gave it to Peter to pack with the rest of the stuff. SOLD!

"You can buy it on Saturday, Claudia," Becca told me. "Otherwise **it won't count** toward our final amount of sales!"

"Sounds good," I said. That was fine with me. I wanted my four dollars added to our rummage sale total. I knew my team would need **every cent** we could get to beat Anna's team.

Finding the Cranky Cat flower pot was **good luck**. But as usual, something not so great happened to even it out.

I ran into Anna and Carly on my way home from Adam's. They were each carrying two shopping bags. The bags were full. I was **EMBARRASSED** that they saw me pulling the empty garden wagon.

"You won't believe the **great** stuff we're getting, Claudia!" Anna exclaimed. She opened a little velvet box to show off a pair of dangly earrings.

"Don't you just love those?" Carly asked.

"They're okay," I said. "I like **pearls** or **gold studs** better."

"Then you should stop by our Boutique booth!" Anna said. "We'll have lots of *cheap,* **boring** earrings in a bargain basket."

Sometimes Anna sounds snotty when she insults me. This time she sounded nice, but it was still an **insult.**

"I'll be too busy selling collectibles at the Tons of Stuff booth," I said.

"Good luck with that," Anna said. She peered into my empty wagon and added, *"You'll need it."*

I heard Anna and Carly giggle as they walked away. They were so sure they would beat us. I was **afraid** they might be right.

My group had found some great stuff. **But was it good enough?**

CHAPTER 6

TREASURE QUEST

I only go to Nick's house when:

1. His mom is paying me to watch him.

2. My mom sends me over to borrow something.

3. It's Halloween.

But on Friday after school, I had to pick up donations to the rummage sale from Nick's mom.

"Come in, Claudia," Mrs. Wright said. "I have a box right over here."

I couldn't wait to see. I was sure she'd have something GREAT to donate. I was hoping she'd give me a bunch of clothes. Her outfits are beautiful, and they always match **perfectly**.

I followed Mrs. Wright into the kitchen. Nick was there, standing by a cardboard box. His arms were folded, and he was frowning.

Nick was not happy.

"She can't have my stuff," Nick said.

When I heard that, I sank down like somebody had let the air out of my tires.

Mrs. Wright was giving me Nick's old things, **not hers.**

I was really disappointed. It would have been so cool to have some **fabulous** clothes that Anna would want to buy.

"Stop pouting," Mrs. Wright said.

I straightened up and smiled, but Mrs. Wright wasn't talking to me.

"You're being *selfish*," Mrs. Wright told Nick.

"I don't care," Nick said. He frowned and stuck out his lower lip.

"These clothes don't fit you anymore," Mrs. Wright said. "Somebody else can use them."

"Claudia can have the clothes," Nick said. "But **she can't have my toys.**"

"Do you play with this?" Mrs. Wright asked. She held up a baby shape-sorting game. "Or these?" She showed us a bag of little plastic people.

Nick yanked the bag of plastic roly-poly people out of his mother's hand. "Don't care," he said. **"They're mine.** You can't sell them."

I've known Nick a long time, so I knew he didn't care about the toddler toys. He just didn't want me to have them.

"What's **really** bugging you, Nick?" I asked, carefully stepping out of kicking distance.

Nick glared at me. "You told me that Old Town was boring," he said. **"It's not.** Matt Morgan said they dress up in costumes and play pioneer with covered wagons and pony rides!"

"They only give pony rides on the weekends," Mrs. Wright said. "And Old Town is boring for a seven-year-old. You'll like it **much better** when you're thirteen."

"I want to go now!" Nick yelled. He stamped his foot.

"No," Mrs. Wright said. "Your dad will take you to the rummage sale instead. But you have to give Claudia the box."

"**Fine,**" Nick said. He kicked the box. He did not unfold his arms or stop pouting. He would not forget, and someday he'd get even.

To get even, he might:

1. Dump dirt in my shoes.

2. Eat the last page of a new book I was reading.

3. Put a frog in the toilet.

I felt better when Mrs. Wright handed me a shopping bag. It was full of scarves and tops, three pairs of new flip-flops, and a bunch of fancy bath products.

I left Mrs. Wright's donations in my front hall with some other things I found in my room to sell.

Dad would be driving me and Adam to school after dinner. **All the groups** were meeting in the gym to set up the booths.

I knew that the Tons of Stuff booth still didn't have any real collectibles, except for Adam's extra comics. I decided to ask Jimmy **one more time**.

I knocked on Jimmy's door.

"**Go away!**" he yelled.

I walked in. "You owe me a favor," I said.

"For what?" Jimmy asked. He didn't turn to look at me. He stared at the game on his computer screen.

"I gave you ponies and doll clothes for your seventh-grade rummage sale," I said. "You must have **something cool** to give me."

Jimmy sighed. "If I give you something, will you leave me alone?" he asked.

"Probably," I said.

"Fine. I have some duplicate Emerald Emperor cards," Jimmy said. "**They aren't rare**, but someone might pay ten dollars for the whole box."

"I'll take it!" I exclaimed. All the boys at Pine Tree Middle School played **Emerald Emperor**. Someone would definitely buy the cards.

"I'll give them to you later," Jimmy said. "If I stop playing now, **I'll lose** points."

"Okay," I said.

I rushed out before Jimmy changed his mind.

Jimmy didn't bring the box of cards when he came down for dinner. And he didn't go back upstairs to get them after we finished eating. He headed for the front door.

"Where are you going?" I asked.

"Out," Jimmy said. "And I'm **late**."

"But I need those cards tonight," I said.

Jimmy looked at his watch. He said, "Take the green box in the corner of my closet." Then he RUSHED out the door.

I ran to Jimmy's room. There were two green boxes in his closet.

The bright green plastic box on the shelf was **almost full** of cards.

The army-green metal box on the floor was dented, and it was only a quarter full.

That was probably the one Jimmy meant, since it had fewer cards.

I took the metal box.

CHAPTER 7

SETTING UP

Our friends were waiting outside when Adam and I got to school. Everyone helped carry boxes into the gym.

"Where's our booth?" I asked.

Tommy pointed at the far wall. "Over there," he said. "Next to Anna's **Fantastic Fashion Boutique**."

My stomach gurgled. It does that sometimes when I'm upset or nervous. "Great," I said. "So we'll be able to hear Anna **BRAG** if her booth is busier than ours."

"There's only one way to fix that," Monica said.

"We'll have to sell **a lot of stuff**," **Becca** said.

"Good plan," I said. "Let's get busy."

Each group had two long tables and two metal shelf units. The booths were six feet apart.

"Do we have room for everything?" I asked nervously.

"Yep," Monica said. "I've got it all **figured out**."

I hoped so. I glanced over at Anna's booth. They seemed really **organized**.

Anna and her friends had brought extra racks for their clothes. Carly and Anna hung dresses and shirts on the bars. The other girls put bags, shoes, and hats on the shelves. Folded clothes, accessories, and several Bargain Baskets sat on the tables.

"Where do we **start**?" Adam asked.

"Books, clothes, and large things on the shelves," Monica said. "**Cool stuff** on the tables. In the front, put out anything that will make people stop to look."

"Like the **lava lamp** and Teddy Bear bookends," Becca said.

"Or the chili pepper clock my mom gave," Tommy said. "It tells the time in Spanish and shouts Ole!"

"Jimmy gave me Emerald Emperor cards," I said.

Adam's head jerked around. **"I want those,"** he said quickly.

"For ten bucks?" I asked. "My brother said the box is worth it."

"**I'll take it,**" Adam said.

"Can I be the cashier?" Sylvia asked.

Adam, Tommy, and Peter unpacked the boxes. Becca and I put the most 𝕀ℕ𝕋𝔼ℝ𝔼𝕊𝕋𝕀ℕ𝔾 things on the tables.

We sorted the rest into boxes. Then we put the boxes under the tables for people to look through. Sylvia and Monica put price tags on the new things we'd brought.

"Look, Claudia," Adam said, setting the Cranky Cat flower pot on the bottom shelf. "You'll be our first sale tomorrow."

"Four dollars will get us off to a **great start,**" Becca said.

"That won't be enough to beat us," Anna called. She stopped hanging jewelry on a table rack at the **Fantastic Fashion Boutique** and walked over. She looked at our table and said, "You won't make much selling this junk."

Just then, Jenny Pinski walked up, pulling a wagon.

Anna frowned. "You're late, Jenny," she said. She sounded annoyed.

Jenny shrugged. "I'm here now, and I brought some stuff to sell," she said. She shoved the wagon handle at Anna.

Anna looked in the wagon. Her nose wrinkled in a sneer. I could tell Anna wasn't impressed with Jenny's donations. In fact, she looked DISGUSTED.

What did Jenny bring? I wondered. *Old sneakers? Broken toys? Rusty pots and pans?*

"You can put prices on it," Jenny told Anna. "I'm going to the movies. See you tomorrow."

Anna didn't argue. She looked relieved. After Jenny left the gym, Anna pushed the wagon under a table. **Then she covered it with a sheet.**

CHAPTER 8

JENNY'S REVENGE

Everyone showed up **early** the next morning. The seventh grade had turned the Pine Tree Middle School Gym into a giant flea market.

"Anna's booth looks like a store in the mall," Monica said. "We look like a thrift store."

"With **too much junk**," Becca added.

"That's okay," I said. I was excited about the rummage sale. I wasn't going to let Anna **spoil it**. "We're selling stuff to pay for the field trip," I added. "It doesn't matter if Anna and her friends make more money."

"You're right," Adam agreed. **"But let's try to beat them anyway."**

Tommy's dad brought doughnuts. He promised to come back later to buy us lunch. The teachers were selling hot dogs, chips, and sodas in the cafeteria.

Peter helped Monica hang a Tons of Stuff banner on the wall. Then Monica hung another sign on the shelves. It said:

Make an offer! We'll probably take it!

Sylvia used a small folding table as a cashier stand. She had a cash box, a calculator, $20.00 in change, and the inventory notebook.

When people began to wander in, we were ready.

Nick and his dad were our first customers.

"Where are my toys?" Nick demanded. He looked **upset**, as usual.

"He wants to buy them back," his father explained. "I don't mind. It's for a **good cause**."

Nick's toys were in a box with some baby stuff Becca had brought. I pulled them out and added up the prices. The total came to $18.00.

"Eighteen dollars?" Nick yelled. He looked shocked.

Mr. Wright gave me a twenty-dollar bill. Then his cell phone rang. After he hung up, he looked at me. "I need a **huge favor**, Claudia," he said nervously.

I knew what that meant. **A huge favor = watch Nick.**

"Would you be able to watch Nick for a little while?" Mr. Wright asked.

"I had a **feeling** that was what you were going to say," I said.

"I don't want to stay here!" Nick complained.

"I've got an EMERGENCY at work," his dad told him, "and your mom isn't home."

"You can have a doughnut," Peter said.

"And help us sell stuff," Becca added.

My friends know Nick. **Bribery always works.**

"Okay!" Nick said.

I gave Mr. Wright his $2.00 change. Then he left. When Mr. Wright was gone, Nick put his toys in a pile and sat down to sell them.

I ate a doughnut while we waited for more customers. Anna's Fantastic Fashion Boutique was **already busy.** Right away, they sold a sundress for $10.00 and Carly's pink Carolina sandals for $5.00.

In our booth, Becca sold Mrs. Arnold's 4th of July potholder for $1.00.

Things did not look good for the Tons of Stuff group.

Then Jenny Pinski arrived. Suddenly, things looked worse for Anna and her friends.

Jenny noticed that none of her donations were on display. *"Where's my stuff?"* she asked Anna. "None of my stuff is on the shelves."

Then Jenny found her wagon under the table, still covered with a sheet. She looked **very angry**. Her face turned bright red.

This is it, I thought. *The moment everyone has been dreading since kindergarten.*

Jenny Pinski was stomping mad, and *she was going to stomp Anna Dunlap.*

I held my breath.

But Jenny was not in a stomping mood. Instead, she pulled her wagon over to our booth. Anna was too busy to notice.

"Do you guys want my stuff?" Jenny asked.

"Sure!" Tommy said. He didn't ask what was in the wagon. "We'll find room for it."

"That's why I'm getting rid of all this," Jenny said. "*No room in my room.* From now on I'm only collecting things from my favorite movies."

"Thanks," Peter said. "We **really** appreciate it."

Jenny smiled as she walked away.

"Guys," Monica whispered. She stared into the wagon. "This is amazing."

We all crowded around the wagon to look.

It was full of video games, movie DVDs and CDs, comic books, action figures, and old Halloween costumes. Some of the things were still in their original packages.

Jenny had given us a collectible jackpot!

CHAPTER 9

SALE-A-THON

We cleared space on a table for Jenny's stuff. Then we got **really busy really fast**.

My next customer was a fifth-grade boy.

"How much do you want for this?" The boy pointed to Jenny's Space Police robot. "There's **no price** on it."

"There isn't?" I asked. I frowned. I didn't know how much the toy was worth. I thought three dollars would be **a good price**. But before I could say that, Nick cut me off.

"Ten dollars," Nick told the fifth grader. "Its eyes light up and it makes *spooky sounds*." He pushed buttons on the robot's front and back.

The boy hesitated. "That's a lot of money," he said.

"You can't buy those robots in stores anymore," Nick added.

I took the hint. "Maybe our price is too low," I said.

"No! Ten dollars is fine. **I'll take it**," the boy said. He paid Sylvia $10.00.

"Good job, Nick!" I exclaimed.

"Shouldn't I get some of the money?" Nick asked.

"No," I said. "The money is for our field trip. But I'll let you have another **doughnut**."

A man and a woman walked up to our booth. The woman kept walking and went to Anna's booth, but the man squatted to look in the boxes under the tables at our booth.

"Hey, Melissa!" the man called out. "You won't believe what these kids have!"

"What?" the woman asked. She dropped a pair of flip-flops on Anna's table and came over.

"Do you want these?" Anna called out.

"No, thanks!" Melissa called back. "What is it, Jack?"

"Old 78 records!" Jack said. He pulled out the box. **"This is great!** How much are these?"

Becca rushed over. "They're a dollar each," she said.

Jack counted the records in the box. "Twenty-four," he said. "Will you take twenty dollars for all of them?"

"Yes, we will," Becca said.

"Great!" Melissa said. She told Becca, "Jack has an old record player. It was his great-grandmother's."

"And now we have records to play on it," Jack said, smiling. He paid Sylvia $20.00.

I was thrilled. When I looked over at Anna, I could tell she wasn't happy. She was mad because she lost a customer to us.

Nick tugged on my shirt. "Can I have a pen?" he asked. "I want to make my prices higher."

He was having fun making money. I gave him a pen and some price stickers.

"How much are these cute little cats?" a lady asked me. I sold her Mrs. Pike's glass cats for $8.00.

Then I heard Anna SQUEAL. "Please, buy something from me, Daddy!" Anna begged.

Her dad was standing at their booth. "I want to help pay for the field trip, Anna," Mr. Dunlap said, "but you don't have anything I want. Don't worry. I'll find something **somewhere else**."

Anna crossed her arms and frowned when her father left. She was furious when he stopped to look though our boxes. She turned bright red when Mr. Dunlap bought all of Adam's tools.

It was the high point of Adam's day.

The high point of **my day** was when I almost sold bicycle spoke lights to Brad Turino.

I had just finished selling some comic books to some little boys when Brad walked up to our booth.

"How's it going, Claudia?" Brad asked.

"Uh, it's — uh . . . good," I stammered.

I get **so flustered** when I'm with Brad that I can't talk. I never get tongue-tied unless he's around.

"We're doing great at the Sports Spot booth," Brad told me. "I'm just taking a break."

"Oh," I said.

My voice sounded WEIRD, so I cleared my throat.

Brad looked through some stuff on our table. He picked up a package. "Spoke flashers!" he exclaimed. "Is this the right price? Only two dollars?"

I nodded. Just then, Nick poked me in the side. "I have to go to the bathroom," he whined.

"Now?" I asked. "**You can wait**, can't you?"

"No!" Nick yelled. He jiggled and shifted from foot to foot.

I sighed. Then I took Nick to the bathroom, and Monica sold Brad the spoke lights. But at least I got to **sort of talk to him** for a minute.

CHAPTER 10

THE JIMMY PROBLEM

Sales at the Tons of Stuff booth were AMAZING! By the end of the day, we had made **$217.35.** But was it more than the Fantastic Fashion Boutique made? I went over to ask.

"So, how much money did you make today?" I asked Anna.

"I can't tell you, Claudia," Anna said. "We haven't added up our money yet."

I didn't believe her. Neither did my friends.

"They lost," **Adam** said. "That's why Anna won't tell."

Monica thought so too. She also thought Anna was going to cheat. "Anna knows how much we made," Monica said. "Now her team will buy just enough stuff to **make sure** they have more."

"They'd better do it fast," Peter said. He pointed.

I looked over to see what he was pointing at. The seventh-grade teachers were collecting the cash boxes.

Sylvia gave **Ms. Stark** our money and the list of things we'd sold. Then Ms. Stark walked to Anna's booth.

"Some people are still looking," Anna told Ms. Stark. "We might make a **few more dollars** for the field trip."

"All the booths are **closed**, Anna," Ms. Stark said. "It's been a **long day**, and everyone wants to go home."

Carly gave Ms. Stark their money and list.

The teachers were going to count the money. Principal Paul would announce the totals on Monday.

I didn't mind waiting. When Ms. Stark turned her back, Anna stuck her tongue out at me. **I was sure we had beaten her.**

Some kids decided to take their unsold stuff home. My team voted to give ours to the Animal Shelter Thrift Store. Even Nick pitched in to help us pack up.

"Did you sell all your toys, Nick?" Adam asked.

Nick nodded. "I made six dollars more than Dad paid Claudia," he said.

"That's almost as cool as **Adam's big sale** to Anna's dad," Tommy exclaimed.

Adam grinned. "Mr. Dunlap bought all my tools and the lava lamp," he said.

Most of my donations sold.

1. A woman bought all of the craft kits for the Senior Center.

2. Mr. Gomez paid full price for the desktop golf game.

3. A man wanted the old coffee pot for camping out.

All of us had bought things at the sale, too.

Tommy found a **dribble mug** that was a practical joke. When someone tried to drink out of it, the mug would drop water down the person's shirt.

"Now my cousin will be sorry he put flies in my raisin bran last summer!" Tommy told us, laughing.

"Did you eat any flies?" I asked.

"I don't know," Tommy said. "Probably."

Becca pretended to gag. "Gross!" she said.

Becca had bought a wooden art box with a palette
and brushes. "It's just like the ones **real
artists** use," she said. "I don't have to mix
my paints on an old plate any more."

Monica couldn't resist a tote bag with a sparkly
unicorn design and a horseshoe candy dish. **She's
horse crazy.**

I loved the Cranky Cat flower pot I bought for
my grandma, but Adam was the most thrilled.
He couldn't wait to sort through **Jimmy's Emerald
Emperor cards.** He had been too busy all day to look
at them.

"Some of my dueling deck cards are pretty beaten
up," Adam said. "I hope there are some good ones in
here." He started to open the metal box, but just then,
his dad came to pick him up.

One by one, everybody left. Monica's mom offered
to take Nick and me home.

"My mom's coming to get us," I said.

Nick and I waited and waited. He counted his money twenty times. Finally, Jimmy finally ran in. **He paused to catch his breath.**

"Please, tell me you didn't sell my Emerald Emperor cards," my brother said. **He looked frantic.**

I told him the truth. "I would if I could but I can't 'cause I did," I said.

"She got ten dollars for them," Nick said.

Jimmy gasped.

"What's the matter?" I asked.

"You took the wrong box," Jimmy said. "You sold **my rare, hard-to-find cards.** They're worth over three hundred dollars!"

CHAPTER 11

PLEA BARGAIN

I felt awful.

No, I felt **worse than awful**. I felt totally terrible. If only things had been different.

1. **If only Jimmy had brought the cards down to dinner.**

2. **If only Jimmy had gotten the cards after dinner.**

3. If only Jimmy had described the box better.

NOTE: All If Onlys are useless because we don't think of them until after we've messed up. Then it's too late.

Jimmy didn't say anything until after we dropped off Nick. Then he said, "You owe me three hundred dollars."

"No, I don't!" I said. I felt stunned. "I didn't take the wrong box **on purpose**," I added.

"You didn't ask if you had the right one," Jimmy insisted.

"You weren't home," I said. "And you didn't check your closet to make sure."

"It's still your fault," my brother said. "You owe me that money, Claudia."

I didn't think I could feel worse than **totally terrible**. But I did. I went straight to my room when we got home. I had $15.00 saved. I put it in my pocket and went to Adam's house.

"Hi, Claudia!" Adam said when he opened the door. He was so happy **he didn't notice that I was miserable**. "You won't believe what's in that box!" he added.

I didn't say anything.

"I can't believe I own a genuine *Green Claw Dragon* card!" Adam exclaimed. "I bet it's worth twenty dollars on its own."

"That's why I'm here," I said.

"It is?" Adam asked. He looked puzzled. "Why?"

"I brought the wrong box to the rummage sale," I explained. "Jimmy meant to give me his duplicate cards to sell. I took his box of **rare cards** by mistake."

"That's too bad," Adam said.

I held out my money. "This is five dollars more than you paid. That's a **good deal**, right?"

"No," Adam said. He shook his head. "I bought the box **fair and square**."

"But Jimmy didn't make the mistake," I explained. "I did."

"Sorry, Claudia. I don't want to sell the cards back," Adam said. He frowned at me. Then he closed the door.

I called Monica as soon as I got home.

"I told Adam that Jimmy didn't mean to give me his **valuable** Emerald Emperor cards. But he wants to keep them anyway," I told her.

"I'm surprised," Monica said. "Adam always **plays fair**."

"I know," I said. "That's why he's been one of my three best friends since third grade." (Monica and Becca are numbers one and two.)

"He sure isn't acting like a **best friend** now," Monica said.

"Maybe he just needs time to think it over," I said. **"Adam always does the right thing."**

"That was before he spent ten bucks to get three hundred dollars worth of Emerald Emperor cards," Monica said. "What if you paid him for them?"

"I tried to give him fifteen dollars," I explained sadly. "It wasn't enough, but it's all I have."

CHAPTER 12

TRUE FRIENDS

Dinner that night was HORRIBLE. Jimmy wouldn't talk to me. He hadn't told my parents what had happened, so they were acting normal.

"How did the rummage sale go?" my father asked.

"Fine," I said. **I didn't look at him.** I just moved food around on my plate.

"You're not eating very much, Claudia," Mom said. "Aren't you hungry after working so hard all day?"

"Not really," I said.

"Did you eat a lot of junk food?" she asked. Her face scrunched up with a worried frown.

"No," I said. To prove it, I ate a piece of **broccoli**.

"Did you sell my CDs and T-shirts?" **Uncle Diego** asked.

"Yes," I told him. I sighed.

Then I realized that everyone was staring at me. They could tell that something was **wrong** because I wasn't going on and on about the rummage sale.

I had two choices: 𝒢𝒰𝒮𝓗 about the sale or **tell them** I sold Jimmy's Emerald Emperor cards for $10.00 by mistake.

I didn't want to talk about Jimmy's cards because:

1. Dad would lecture me about being more careful.

2. Mom would try to get Jimmy and me to make up.

3. Families are fair and pay each other back.

Jimmy didn't say anything for the same reasons, except number 3. Jimmy's number 3 would be:

3. Family is more important than cards or money.

"So, all of my things were sold?" Uncle Diego asked.

"Most of them," I said. "This old guy really liked white T-shirts, and he **didn't care** about the ads. Another guy bought some of the CDs to sell at the real flea market."

"How much did you get?" Uncle Diego asked.

"A dollar each," I said. "Fifty cents for some of the T-shirts."

"Is that all?" Uncle Diego asked. He looked disappointed.

"They sold everything **dirt cheap**," Jimmy mumbled.

My brother was really mad at me. He'd probably stay mad until I was thirty. Maybe longer.

I did not want to spend the rest of my life feeling guilty about a box of stupid cards.

It wasn't **fair**.

It wasn't my **fault**.

But it didn't **matter**.

"Can I be EXCUSED?" I asked.

Mom nodded, and I bolted from the table.

Just then, the phone rang. I answered it. It was Becca.

"Monica told me 𝔼𝕍𝔼ℝ𝕐𝕋ℍ𝕀ℕ𝔾," Becca said. "We think Adam will sell the cards back if you pay him more."

"He might," I said. "But I only have fifteen dollars."

"Monica and I have some money," Becca said. "We want to chip in."

I smiled. Monica and Becca weren't just best friends. They were true friends.

"I'm not sure any amount will be enough," I said. "But thanks so much for the help."

"Just let us know if you need it," Becca said.

"Thanks, Becca," I said.

After we hung up, I sat on the stairs.

I felt **bad** because of Jimmy and Adam and **good** because of Becca and Monica.

It was **weird** to feel both ways at the same time.

Then the phone rang again.

"Hi," Tommy said. "Becca told me **you need some cash**. And she said I can't ask why."

Becca didn't want Adam's guy friends to know he was being a jerk. I didn't either.

"Peter and I can give you some money tomorrow," Tommy said.

"Thanks, Tommy!" I said.

I was astonished. I knew I had great friends. I just never realized that they were **supremely great**!

Right after we hung up, the doorbell rang.

I opened the door and gasped with surprise. **It was Adam.**

"Here," he said. He handed me the metal box. "All the cards are there."

I was shocked.

"You're giving them back?" I asked.

"I can't keep them," Adam explained. "I know Jimmy didn't want to sell them. I should have given them back **right away**."

"You still paid for it," I said. I held out the $15.00.

"I don't want your money, Claudia," Adam said.

Jimmy walked into the living room. He walked over and took the metal box from me. "Do you want the cards **I meant to sell**?" Jimmy asked Adam.

"Yeah!" Adam said. His face lit up. "That would be great."

"Cool," Jimmy said.

Then he opened the metal box and took out a card. He gave it to Adam.

"This is a bonus for **being honest** and returning my cards," Jimmy said.

"*The Green Claw Dragon!*" Adam whispered. He stared at the card. Then he looked up at Jimmy and smiled. "Thanks," Adam said.

My brother and Adam were both happy again, and I felt a hundred times better. Adam was a **true friend** after all.

CHAPTER 13

P.S.

I called Becca back right after Adam left. Nobody had talked to Adam. Bringing the cards back was his idea. He still had a perfect record for **doing the right thing.**

Nick decided he really did want to go to Old Town. First he **threw a fit**. Then he said he'd buy his own ticket with the $24.00 he made at the rummage sale. Finally, his mom agreed. His parents are taking him sometime on the weekend, when Old Town will have pony rides.

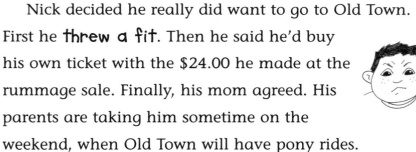

The class made enough money at the rummage sale to pay for the field trip. And the Tons of Stuff booth made more than Anna's Fantastic Fashion Boutique.

WOOHOO!

Nobody broke the school record.

We weren't upset. We'd still done really well.

Jenny hadn't given us her donations to be nice. *She wanted to get back at Anna.* It worked. All together, the stuff we'd sold from Jenny's wagon added up to $35.00. We beat Anna by $23.00. Without Jenny, we might not have been able to do it!

Adam replaced the torn cards in his collection with duplicates from Jimmy's plastic box. There were even a couple of cards he didn't have yet. Plus, he also found a **sort-of-rare** Crystal Wizard card. I told Jimmy. He said that Adam had bought the box **fair and square**. Whatever was in it was his.

My grandma **really loved** the flower pot.

About the Author

Diana G. Gallagher lives in Florida with her husband and five dogs, four cats, and a cranky parrot. Her hobbies are gardening, garage sales, and grandchildren. She has been an English equitation instructor, a professional folk musician, and an artist. However, she had aspirations to be a professional writer at the age of twelve. She has written dozens of books for kids and young adults.

About the Illustrator

Brann Garvey lives in Minneapolis, Minnesota with his wife, Keegan, their dog, Lola, and their very fat cat, Iggy. Brann graduated from Iowa State University with a bachelor of fine arts degree. He later attended the Minneapolis College of Art and Design, where he studied illustration. In his free time, Brann enjoys being with his family and friends. He brings his sketchbook everywhere he goes.

Glossary

accessories (ak-SESS-uh-reez)—things that go with your clothes, like belts or jewelry

challenge (CHAL-uhnj)—invite someone to fight or try to do something

collectibles (cuh-LEKT-ih-buhlz)—things that a person tries to buy many of to gather together

designer (di-ZINE-ur)—made by a famous maker

donate (DOH-nate)—to give away

donation (doh-NAY-shuhn)—something that is given away

educational (ej-uh-KAY-shuhn-uhl)—something that gives knowledge

gloat (GLOHT)—to delight in your own good luck or in someone else's bad luck

rare (RAIR)—not often seen, found, or happening

record (REK-urd)—if you set a record, you do something better than anyone else has

rummage sale (RUM-ij SALE)—a sale of used items

tantrum (TAN-truhm)—an outburst of anger

treasure (TREZH-ur)—something that is valued very highly

Discussion Questions

1. In this book, Claudia's class raises money for a field trip by having a rummage sale. Do you ever have to raise money? What do you raise money for? How do you raise the money? Talk about your answers.

2. Why did Jenny give her rummage sale donations to Claudia's group? How did it help Claudia's group? How do you think Anna felt about it?

3. Besides the things mentioned in this book, what are some other things that people you know collect? What do you collect?

Writing Prompts

1. If you were looking for a collectible at a rummage sale, what would you hope to find? Describe the item, and then draw a picture of it.

2. Nick doesn't want to give up his old toys. Write about your favorite toy from your childhood. What was it? Why did you like it so much? What happened to it?

3. Pretend that you found a rare trading card that was worth $300. What would you use the money for? Write about your answer.

MORE FUN with Claudia!

BEWARE!

THE COMPLICATED LIFE OF

Claudia
Cristina
Cortez

BY DIANA G. GALLAGHER

Claudia Cristina Cortez

Just like every other thirteen-year-old girl, Claudia Cristina Cortez has a complicated life. Whether she's studying for the big Quiz Show, babysitting her neighbor, Nick, avoiding mean Jenny Pinski, planning the seventh-grade dance, or trying desperately to pass the swimming test at camp, Claudia goes through her complicated life with confidence, cleverness, and a serious dash of cool.

David Mortimore Baxter

David is a great kid, but he has one big problem — he can't stop talking. These wildly humorous stories, told by David himself, will show readers just how much trouble a boy and his mouth can get into, whether he's going on a class trip, trying to find a missing neighbor, running a detective agency, or getting lost in the wild. David is amiable, engaging, cool, and smart enough to realize that growing up is the biggest adventure of all.

WAIT!

DON'T close the book!
There's
MORE!

FIND MORE:
Games
Puzzles
Heroes
Villains
Authors
Illustrators at...

www. **capstonekids** .com

Still want MORE?
Find cool websites and more books like this
one at www.Facthound.com.

Just type in the Book ID: 9781434215727
and you're ready to go!